Dear Parent:
Your child's love of reading starts here!

Every child learns to read in a different way and at his or her own speed. Some go back and forth between reading levels and read favorite books again and again. Others read through each level in order. You can help your young reader improve and become more confident by encouraging his or her own interests and abilities. From books your child reads with you to the first books he or she reads alone, there are I Can Read Books for every stage of reading:

SHARED READING
Basic language, word repetition, and whimsical illustrations ideal for sharing with your emergent reader

BEGINNING READING
Short sentences, familiar words, and simple concepts for children eager to read on their own

READING WITH HELP
Engaging stories, longer sentences, and language play for developing readers

READING ALONE
Complex plots, challenging vocabulary, and high-interest topics for the independent reader

ADVANCED READING
Short paragraphs, chapters, and exciting themes for the perfect bridge to chapter books

I Can Read Books have introduced children to the joy of reading since 1957. Featuring award-winning authors and illustrators and a fabulous cast of beloved characters, I Can Read Books set the standard for beginning readers.

A lifetime of discovery begins with the magical words "I Can Read!"

Visit www.icanread.com for information
on enriching your child's reading experience.

I Can Read Book® is a trademark of HarperCollins Publishers.

Pete the Cat: A Pet for Pete
Copyright © 2014 by James Dean
All rights reserved. Printed in the United States of America. No part of this book may be used or reproduced in any manner whatsoever without written permission except in the case of brief quotations embodied in critical articles and reviews. For information address HarperCollins Children's Books, a division of HarperCollins Publishers, 195 Broadway, New York, NY 10007.
www.icanread.com
Library of Congress catalog card number: 2013942066

ISBN 978-0-06-230380-6 (trade bdg.)—ISBN 978-0-06-230379-0 (pbk.)

16 17 18 PC/WOR   10   ❖   First Edition

I Can Read!

SHARED **My First** READING

Pete the Cat

A PET FOR PETE

By James Dean

HARPER

An Imprint of HarperCollinsPublishers

Pete is going to the pet store.

He is going to get a pet.

Pete wants a bird,

a hamster, or a lizard.

But then Pete sees a goldfish.

"That's what I want,"

he tells his mom.

Pete's mom gets fish food.
"I'm going to call you Goldie,"
Pete says to his new pet.

"You are my first pet,"
Pete tells Goldie
on the way home.

Pete takes Goldie to his room.

He feeds her fish food.

"Now what?" asks Pete.

He can't play with Goldie.

He can't swim with her.

Pete knows what he can do!

Pete paints a picture of Goldie.

He paints four fins

and an orange tail.

"What a pretty painting,"
says Pete's mom.
"You can keep it," says Pete.

"Cool painting!" says Bob.
"Can you make one for me?"
"Sure," says Pete.

Pete paints a picture for Bob.

"Wow!" says Bob.

"It looks just like Goldie."

Bob shows Pete's painting
to his friend Tom.
Now Tom wants a painting, too.

Pete paints another picture
of Goldie to take to school
for show-and-tell.

"This is Goldie, my pet fish,"
Pete tells his class.

17

"I wish I had a picture
of Goldie," says Benny.
"I'll make you one," says Pete.

Everyone in Pete's class
wants a painting of Goldie!

Pete's grandma wants
a painting, too.

Pete has a lot to do.

He has to feed Goldie.

He has to do homework.

Pete paints and paints.
He makes paintings for
everyone on his list.

At last Pete is done!

He worked hard.

There is no paint left.

Pete's paintings are a big hit!
Pete is happy to be done.

But Pete is not done.

Now everyone in town

wants a painting of Goldie!

Pete gets more paint.
"I don't know what to do,"
he says to his mom.

"I wish I could paint
pictures for everyone.
I just don't have time."

Pete's mom has an idea!

She tells it to Pete.

"Great idea!" says Pete.

Pete gets right to it.
This time he works outside
and makes a huge painting.

Honk! Honk!

Beep! Beep!

Here comes Pete!

He has made one painting

of Goldie for everyone

in town to enjoy!

What a great day!
When Pete gets home, he tells
the real Goldie all about it.